To Talia
Lovely to See You
Love,
Mama Cheryl
2023

KAYLA'S MAGIC EYES

Niles Love Series

Text Copyright © 2013 by CHERYL HINTON

Illustrations Copyright © 2013 by SEAN COATES

Edited by Althia Melody Ellis

All rights reserved. Printed in USA by Mosaic Paradigm Group, LLC. (www.mpg-publishing.com)

ISBN 978-0-578-11929-8

No part of this book may be reproduced in whole or in part, or transmitted in any form or by any means, written permission from the author.

Kayla's Magic Eyes

Written by Cheryl Hinton
Illustrated by Sean Coates

Word has it……and you are hearing it from me…………….
A long, long time ago and in a very far away place called Nobirdland, lived a little girl named Kayla. Kayla was just a wee five years old. She was a beautiful little girl. In fact, she looked just like….YOU. (That is, if you are a little girl!)

Kayla had the most beautiful eyes just like..............YOU. Her Mom always told her, "Kayla, you have magic eyes!" She was not quite sure what that meant but she knew it had to be something good.

Then her Mom would always give her a big hug and a huge kiss. Kayla would smile the biggest smile and her eyes would become even more beautiful! Wow! Her eyes! Her eyes turned into …..Happy Eyes! What do Happy Eyes look like? Yes….just like that!

Her eyes glistened, glow and sparkled! Her family, friends and even people she didn't know noticed Kayla's magic eyes. They could tell just what she meant by her magic eyes.

On a clear, beautiful day, Kayla could not go out to play because she had a cold. She got so sad! Her eyes became so sad. Kayla thought her magic eyes, as well as her heart, would not be happy again. Sniff, sniff.....achoo!!

Well….the next day she felt better and went outside to play. Her Mom was making a cake but she did not have any eggs. Her Mom called her and said, "Kayla, please go to the store and get me one egg." Kayla was excited. She felt like a big girl because she was going to the store all by herself. Suddenly her magic eyes turned to what? HAPPY EYES! (You may be wondering how she could go to the store by herself……………the store was right next to her house!)

Kayla went out of her yard, to the sidewalk, around the fence,

down the sidewalk, up the steps,

right into the store!

Whew! What a walk!

Kayla and her happy eyes greeted Mr. Moe, the grocer. "Hi Mr. Moe!" Kayla said. "My Mom needs one egg for her cake, please", she sang. "No problem!" Mr. Moe sang back to her.

Whistling, Mr. Moe went to his back yard, lifted up a chicken and magically removed a perfect egg! Yes! An egg! "Here you go, Kayla! Be careful. It's a fresh egg!" Mr. Moe warned. Kayla opened her hand carefully, gently wrapped her fingers around the egg, and headed back to her Mom.

Kayla was so happy. She skipped out of the store, down the steps, down the sidewalk
and almost, almost got around the fence when suddenly, out of nowhere……………she…………………she………………she……………fell!

And the egg……………"OH NO! THE EGG! It smashed right on the ground, right under her nose.
Oh……………Kayla's eyes became so sad again!

But something else happened. Her happy, magical eyes became full of tears. Her gorgeous eyes cried so many tears, that a puddle formed all around the smashed egg. OH NO! Poor Kayla!

"What will Mommy say?" Kayla thought. "I am a big girl, I can't tell her! I know what I'll do!" Kayla decided. Kayla's teary eyes started to dry. Her eyes got bigger as she thought of the story to tell her Mom. She did not want her to know she destroyed the egg. After all, she did not want to disappoint her Mom.

OH NO! Kayla was not going to tell the truth! Her magic eyes got even bigger and wider as she thought of how to cover up her accident. So, she got up and dusted herself off, picked up a stick and quickly covered the egg with dirt. Though her eyes became bigger, there was no sparkle to be seen.

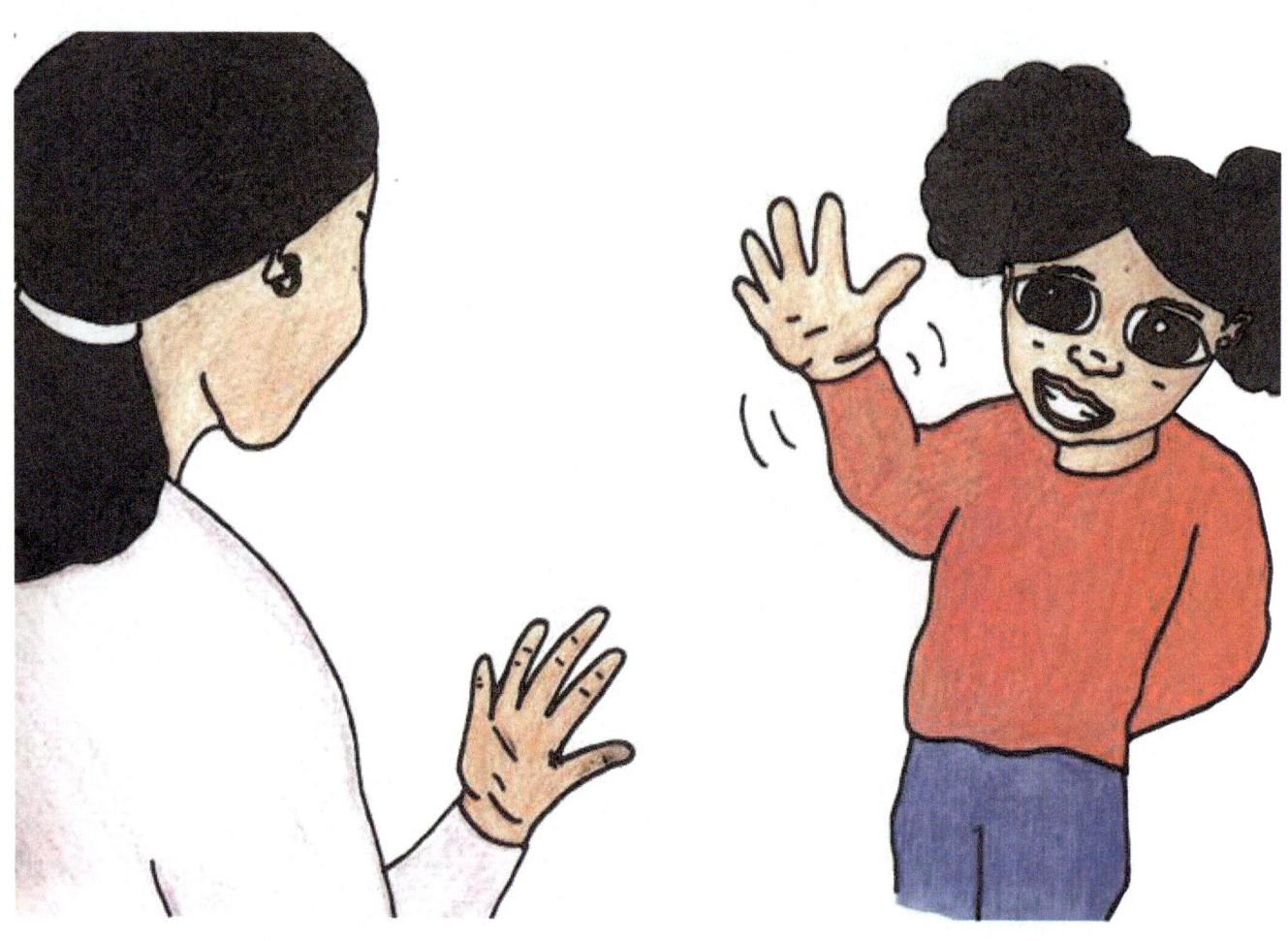

Kayla walked home and went to the kitchen. "Hi Mom........how's it going?" Kayla's eyes were beginning to get big. "Hey Kayla", her Mom who had been waiting patiently answered, "Where's the egg from Mr. Moe?"

Kayla took a deep breath and began her story. "Well, I got it but a big bird swooped down and snatched it. Then, the big bird dropped it from the sky and it smashed into the dirt!" Kayla eyes were so big and so wide that she could not blink her eyes! Her Mom's eyes became the opposite as Kayla told her story.

She tried to blink but it just would not happen. Her Mom looked at her so strangely and asked, "Kayla! What are you talking about? And what is going on with your eyes?"
"OH NO!" Kayla thought.

"Let's go back to Mr. Moe's and ask him about this BIG BIRD!"

Kayla was so scared. This had never happened to her before. Her eyes had gotten bigger and she could not blink her eyes. She had…………magical eyes! It would have been so much easier to just tell the truth.

They went out of their yard, to the sidewalk, around the fence, down the sidewalk, up the steps and right into store. Her Mom asked Mr. Moe if he saw a great BIG bird swoop down on Kayla. Kayla's eyes were enormous and they still did not blink!
Mr. Moe said,
"Kayla, there are no birds in NOBIRDLAND.
Not ones that fly! WE only have chickens!"

Kayla never told the truth so she never blinked her magic eyes again. It would have been so much easier to just tell the truth.

So remember...whenever you think you might not want to tell the truth, think about Kayla's magic eyes.

Check yourself to make sure you can blink your eyes.

Can you blink your eyes? Just checking!

CHERYL HINTON
Storyteller
Cheryl Hinton is a member of the Griot Circle of Maryland, National Association of Black Storytellers and Wombwork Productions, Inc. She is also co-founder of Mama Talk, a storytelling duo and previously co-hosted a Maryland Public Television show called the Talking Drum. Her stories are woven with virtues, morals, civility and guide imagination into places where we all need to be every day, in every way ~ living and breathing God's Love. Not only is she a storyteller, she is a dancer, poet, singer, actress, costumer and veteran of several Baltimore-based African Dance Companies. She has facilitated workshops on various educational and diversity topics as well instructed African dance and physical fitness for children and adults. In her travels throughout the USA and diverse destinations of the Caribbean, West and East Africa, she tells stories and dances to the rhythm of life.

Love, as she is affectionately known by her grandson, is the Dansa Griot, one who embraces the gift of the spoken word, song and traditional dance as a healing art of our people.

SEAN COATES
Illustrator
Graphic Designer, Illustrator and Artist. Sean's creative, illustrative abilities and crafty thoughts and ideas have innately gifted him from a young age. Inspired by his High School Art Teacher, he followed his artistic passions and attended the Art Institution of Washington where he received his BFA in Fine Arts with a focus on Graphic Design. He began his career as a Graphic Designer in the Press Printing Industry and later elevated his skillsets with the United States Department of State where he worked as a Designer in Publishing. Sean also is a Freelance Artist in apparel designs, print text and illustrating children's books.

Acknowledgements

*Giving All Honor to the Most High, the Magnificent.
I am most grateful
for the journey for the best is yet to come.
Thank you to my family for allowing me
to dream by biggest dreams.
To my nephew Sean, for sharing your creative
talent and to my grandson Nile, this is for you….*

All that God is,

Is in You.

GOD is Love

And always know that

LOVE loves YOU.

Kayla's Magic Eyes

Niles' Love series

©2001

CPSIA information can be obtained
at www.ICGtesting.com
Printed in the USA
BVOW07*2033060317
477900BV00001B/1/P